A CHRISTMAS OF RENEWED FAITH

KAYLA LOWE

Copyright © 2024 by Kayla Lowe

All rights reserved.

No part of this book may be reproduced in any form or by any electronic or mechanical means, including information storage and retrieval systems, without written permission from the author, except for the use of brief quotations in a book review.

Want a free book? Sign up to my newsletter to get my award-winning book for free! www.authorkaylalowe.com

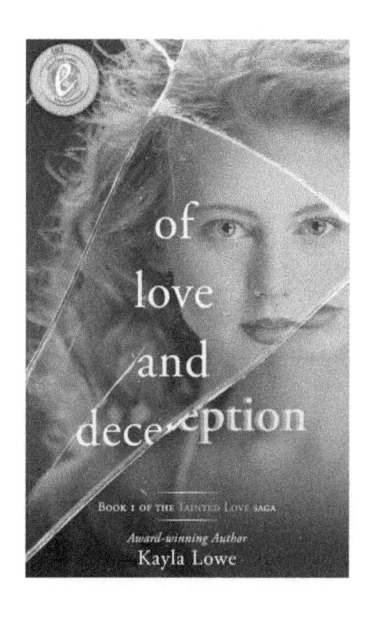

MORE OF MY BOOKS

Series

Women of the Bible Fiction

Ruth
Esther
Rachel
Hannah
Deborah

❋

Charms of the Chaste Court

A Courtship in Covent Garden
Whispers in Westminster
Romance in Regent's Park
Serenade on Strand Street
Treasure in Tower Bridge

❋

Sweet Honey by the Sea

The Beekeeper's Secret (Book 1)
A Royal Honeycomb (Book 2)
Bees in Blossom (Book 3)

<u>Honeyed Kisses (Book 4)</u>
<u>Blooming Forever (Book 5)</u>

❋

<u>Strawberry Beach Series</u>

<u>Beachside Lessons (Book 1)</u>
<u>Beachside Lessons (Book 2)</u>
<u>Beachside Lessons (Book 3)</u>

❋

Panama City Beach Series

Sun-Kissed Secrets (Book 1)
Sun-Kissed Secrets (Book 2)
Sun-Kissed Secrets (Book 3)

❋

The Tainted Love Saga

Of Love and Deception (Book 1)
Of Love and Family (Book 2)
Of Love and Violence (Book 3)
Of Love and Abuse (Book 4)
Of Love and Crime (Book 5)
Of Love and Addiction (Book 6)
Of Love and Redemption (Book 7)

❋

Standalones

Maiden's Blush

❄

Poetry

Phantom Poetry
Lost and Found

1

Milly's breath formed small puffs of fog in the crisp December air as she stepped out of her car and gazed up at the white steeple of Cedar Ridge Community Church. The sight was at once familiar and foreign, a bittersweet reminder of the life she'd left behind. She pulled her coat tighter around her shoulders and made her way up the worn stone steps.

Inside, the church was awash in the warm glow of string lights and the sweet aroma of pine garlands. Milly paused in the entryway, taking in the festive decorations and the low murmur of friendly chatter among the congregation members milling about. Her mother spotted her from across the room and hurried over, arms outstretched.

"Milly, you made it! Oh, it's so good to see you, sweetheart." Her mother enveloped her in a tight hug, the scent of cinnamon and vanilla enveloping Milly like a comforting blanket.

"Hi, Mom. It's good to be back," Milly said softly, returning the embrace. She blinked back the sudden sting of tears, surprised by the swell of emotion that rose in her throat.

Her mother stepped back, hands still resting on Milly's shoulders, and studied her face with a knowing look. "I'm so glad you decided to come home for Christmas. It just wouldn't be the same without you."

Milly managed a small smile. "I wasn't sure if I was ready, but...I think I need this. To be here, to remember what Christmas used to mean to me."

Her mother squeezed her shoulders gently. "You're exactly where you're meant to be, dear. Now, let's find a good seat before the service begins!"

As they made their way into the sanctuary, Milly couldn't help but feel a flicker of hope amid the lingering ache in her heart. Maybe coming home was the first step in finding her way back to the faith and joy she'd once known.

As Milly entered the sanctuary beside her mother, a wave of nostalgia washed over her. The polished wooden pews gleamed in the soft light, and the air was filled with the gentle murmur of the congregation. She breathed in deeply, catching the scent of beeswax candles mingling with the fragrance of evergreen boughs that adorned the altar.

Memories flooded back, unbidden—Christmases past spent in this very church, singing carols and listening to messages of hope and love. James had always been by her side then, his hand warm in hers as they celebrated the joy of the season together. The thought of him sent a sharp pang through her chest, and she swallowed hard against the lump that rose in her throat.

It had been two years since his death, but the pain still felt fresh at times like these. In the aftermath of his passing, Milly had fled Cedar Ridge and the reminders of their life together, seeking solace in the anonymity of the city. She'd thrown herself into her work as a graphic designer, trying to lose herself in the bustle and noise of urban life. But even as she'd built a new routine for herself, she'd felt adrift, disconnected from the faith and community that had once been her anchor.

Now, as she slid into a pew beside her mother and looked up at the cross that hung above the altar, Milly felt a stirring of something long-dormant within her. The familiar words of the opening hymn washed over her, and she found herself mouthing along to the lyrics almost without thinking.

"O come, all ye faithful, joyful and triumphant..."

The voices of the congregation rose around her, and Milly felt a sudden rush of tears prick at the corners of her eyes. She blinked them back, determined not to let her emotions overtake her. But as the music swelled and the lights twinkled on the Christmas tree in the corner, she couldn't help but feel a sense of homecoming.

Maybe her mother was right—maybe this was exactly where she needed to be right now. Not running from her grief, but facing it head-on, in the company of those who loved and supported her. As the pastor began to speak, Milly settled back in her seat and let the familiar words of scripture wash over her, feeling for the first time in a long time that perhaps there was still hope to be found, even in the darkest of times.

2

Noah stood at the window of his workshop, gazing out at the snow-dusted streets of Cedar Ridge. He let out a heavy sigh, his breath fogging up the glass. Behind him, a half-finished rocking horse waited on the workbench, a tangible reminder of all he needed to do before Christmas.

"Daddy?" A small voice from the doorway drew his attention. He turned to see Lily standing there in her favorite reindeer pajamas, her blonde curls tousled from sleep.

"Hey there, Lil." He crossed the room and scooped her up in his arms. "What are you doing out of bed?"

She looped her arms around his neck, nestling

her head against his shoulder. "I couldn't sleep. I was thinking 'bout the Christmas play."

Noah's heart clenched. The church Christmas play had always been a highlight for their family, but since his wife's passing, he'd found it hard to muster any enthusiasm for the holidays.

Noah carried Lily over to the old leather armchair in the corner of the workshop and settled her on his lap. She snuggled against his chest as he gently stroked her hair, his mind drifting to memories of Christmases past.

He could still vividly picture Colleen's radiant smile as she stood on the stage, directing the children in their roles for the nativity scene. Her laughter would ring out like silver bells, filling the church with joy and warmth. Noah's heart ached at the thought of never again seeing her eyes sparkle with merriment or feeling her arms wrap around him in a loving embrace.

Lily's small hand reached up to touch his cheek, drawing him back to the present. "Daddy, you're crying," she whispered, her own eyes glistening with concern.

Noah hastily wiped away the tears he hadn't realized had fallen. "I'm okay, sweetheart. I just miss your mommy, especially this time of year."

"I miss her too," Lily said softly, burying her face against his flannel shirt. "Do you think she's watching over us from heaven?"

A lump formed in Noah's throat as he hugged his daughter closer. "I know she is, Lil. Your mommy loved you more than anything in this world, and that love doesn't just go away." He took a shaky breath, trying to steady his voice. "She'd want us to remember the happy times and to keep making new memories, even though it's hard without her here."

Lily nodded solemnly, her little fingers playing with the buttons on his shirt. "Maybe we could make a special ornament for the Christmas tree, just for Mommy. That way she'll always be with us when we celebrate."

Tears pricked at Noah's eyes once more, but this time they were accompanied by a bittersweet smile. "That's a wonderful idea, honey. We'll make the most beautiful ornament for her, and every time we see it on the tree, we'll think of all the love and joy she brought into our lives."

As he held his daughter close, Noah felt a flicker of warmth amidst the grief that had been his constant companion these past two years. Colleen may be gone from this earth, but her love lived on through Lily—through the precious child they had created together. He knew that as long as he had Lily, he would always carry a piece of Colleen in his heart.

It was just hard to attend the Christmas play, what with all the memories he had of Colleen.

Still, he knew how much it meant to Lily.

"About the play," he began. "I was thinking maybe we could help out with the play this year. What do you say?"

Lily's face lit up. "Really? You mean it, Daddy?"

He brushed a stray curl from her forehead and smiled. "I do. I know it's been tough since Mommy...since she's been gone. But I think she'd want us to keep the Christmas spirit alive."

"She loved Christmas." Lily's voice was soft, tinged with a wisdom beyond her years.

"She did." Noah swallowed past the lump in his throat. "And she loved you, so much. So, let's do this, for her and for each other. Okay?"

Lily nodded, a determined look settling on her small features. "Okay."

He hugged her close, feeling a flicker of something he hadn't felt in a long time—hope, and perhaps the faintest whisper of renewed faith.

Maybe this Christmas would be the turning point they both needed.

With a newfound sense of resolve, Noah gently set Lily on her feet. "Come on, little miss. Let's get you back to bed. We've got a big day tomorrow, picking out the perfect tree and making that special ornament for Mommy."

3

The bell above the diner door jingled merrily as Milly stepped inside, a gust of frigid air following her. She stamped the snow from her boots, breathing in the comforting aroma of coffee and freshly baked pie. It was as if no time had passed at all since she'd last been here.

As she unwound her scarf, her gaze landed on a familiar figure seated at the counter. Noah Boyle, his dark hair now peppered with gray at the temples, was cradling a steaming mug between his hands. Her heart stuttered. She hadn't seen him since...well, since before everything changed.

Milly hesitated, debating whether to slip quietly into a booth, but Noah chose that moment to glance up. His blue eyes widened in recognition, and a tentative smile tugged at his lips.

"Milly? Milly Cook?" He stood, closing the distance between them in a few long strides. "I almost didn't recognize you."

She laughed softly, tucking a strand of hair behind her ear. "It's been a long time."

"Too long." Noah's smile was warm, tinged with a hint of sadness that Milly understood all too well. "I heard you were back in town. It's good to see you."

"You too." And it was. Standing there, looking into the face of someone who'd known her before the city, before the grief, Milly felt a sense of comfort wash over her. "I'm just here for the holidays, helping Mom out."

Noah nodded. "Same here. Well, not with your mom, obviously." He chuckled, rubbing the back of his neck. "I'm helping with the church play. Lily's idea."

"The Christmas play?" Memories flooded back, of happier times, of laughter and carols and the warmth of community. "That's wonderful. I'm sure Lily's thrilled."

"She is. It's been...hard, since her mom..." He trailed off, a shadow crossing his features.

Milly's heart ached for him. She reached out, laying a hand on his arm. "I'm so sorry, Noah. I heard about your wife. I can't imagine how difficult it's been."

He covered her hand with his own, his palm rough and warm. "Thank you. It hasn't been easy, but Lily, she's my light. And this play, it's bringing back some of the joy we've been missing."

They stood like that for a moment, connected by shared grief and understanding. Finally, Noah cleared his throat. "Listen, I know you just got back, but would you maybe want to grab a coffee sometime? Catch up properly?"

Milly found herself nodding, a smile spreading across her face. "I'd like that."

"Great." Noah's answering smile was brighter than the twinkling Christmas lights strung along the diner's walls. "I'm looking forward to it."

As they exchanged numbers and made plans to meet later in the week, Milly felt a flicker of something she hadn't felt in a long time—anticipation, and perhaps the faintest stirring of her long-dormant faith. Maybe this Christmas would be the turning point she needed.

❄

The week flew by in a flurry of activity. Milly found herself swept up in the familiar rhythms of small-town life—helping her mother bake cookies for the church bazaar, catching up with old friends over steaming mugs of cocoa, and watching the town square transform into a winter wonderland of twinkling lights and festive decorations.

Through it all, the promise of her upcoming coffee date with Noah lingered in the back of her mind, a bright spot amidst the bittersweet nostalgia. When the day finally arrived, Milly found herself standing in front of her closet, suddenly unsure of what to wear. She settled on a cozy cream-colored sweater and dark jeans, hoping to strike a balance between casual and put-together.

The little café on Main Street was warm and inviting, with the rich aroma of roasted coffee beans and the soft strains of holiday music filling the air. Milly spotted Noah immediately, seated at a table by the window. He stood as she approached, his smile lighting up his handsome face.

"Milly, hi." He pulled out a chair for her, ever the gentleman. "I'm so glad you could make it."

"Me too." She settled into the seat, shrugging

out of her coat. "This place is lovely. I don't remember it being here before."

"It's new," Noah explained, reclaiming his own chair. "Opened up last year. They have the best peppermint mocha in town."

Milly grinned. "Well, I'll have to try one of those, then."

As they placed their orders and fell into easy conversation, Milly marveled at how natural it felt to be here with Noah. They talked about their lives, their work, and the changes they'd both gone through. Noah spoke of his daughter with such love and pride that Milly's heart melted.

"She sounds like an amazing little girl," she said softly.

Noah's smile was tinged with sadness. "She is. She's the reason I get up every morning. After losing Colleen, I didn't know how I'd go on. But Lily, she needs me. And being there for her, it's helped me heal, too."

Milly nodded. "I understand. After James died, I thought I'd never find my way out of the darkness. But little by little, day by day, it gets a little easier to breathe."

Noah nodded back. "It does. And having

people who understand, who've been through it too, that helps."

Milly reached across the table, her fingers brushing Noah's hand in a comforting gesture. "It really does. I'm so glad we ran into each other, Noah. Talking to you, it feels...right. Like maybe coming back to Cedar Ridge was exactly what I needed."

Noah's eyes met hers, warm and understanding. "I know what you mean. Having you here, it's brought back memories I thought I'd lost. Good ones, from before everything changed."

They sat in comfortable silence for a moment, sipping their coffees and watching the snow drift lazily past the window. Finally, Noah set down his mug, a thoughtful expression on his face.

"Listen, Milly, I know this might be a lot to ask, but would you consider helping out with the Christmas play? We could really use an artistic eye for the sets and costumes."

Milly hesitated, old fears and doubts creeping in. It had been so long since she'd let herself create anything, let alone something for the community she'd left behind. But looking at Noah's hopeful face, she felt a stirring of something long dormant—a desire to reconnect, to find purpose again.

"You know what? I'd love to help." The words tumbled out before she could second-guess herself, and the answering smile on Noah's face made her heart flutter.

"Really? That's fantastic! Lily will be thrilled, and I...well, I'm really looking forward to working with you."

Milly grinned, feeling lighter than she had in years. "Me too, Noah. I think this is exactly what I need right now."

As they finished their coffees and made plans for Milly to come by the church later in the week, she couldn't help but marvel at the unexpected turn her life had taken. Coming back to Cedar Ridge, facing the ghosts of her past, it had seemed an insurmountable challenge. But with Noah by her side and a new sense of purpose blooming in her heart, Milly felt a glimmer of hope that maybe, just maybe, this Christmas would be the start of something wonderful.

4

The next few days passed in a whirlwind of activity as Milly threw herself into helping with the Christmas play. She spent hours at the church, painting backdrops, sewing costumes, and brainstorming ideas with Noah and the other volunteers. It was exhilarating to be creating again, to watch her visions come to life in bold strokes of color and fabric.

But more than that, it was the sense of community, of being part of something bigger than herself, that truly warmed Milly's heart. Watching the children rehearse their lines, seeing the joy and excitement on their faces, it reminded her of the faith and hope she'd once held so dear.

And then there was Noah. Working side by

side with him, laughing over silly mishaps and sharing quiet moments of understanding, Milly felt a connection growing between them. It was different from anything she'd experienced before, a sense of comfort and familiarity that seemed to flow effortlessly. She found herself looking forward to their conversations, to the way his eyes crinkled at the corners when he smiled.

One afternoon, as they were putting the finishing touches on the manger scene, Noah turned to Milly with a thoughtful expression. "You know, I've been meaning to thank you," he said softly.

Milly looked up from the straw she was arranging, surprised. "Thank me? For what?"

"For everything you've done here. For bringing your talent and your heart to this project. It means more than you know." His gaze held hers, warm and sincere.

Milly felt a flush rise to her cheeks. "I'm just happy to help," she demurred. "It's been wonderful to be a part of this, to feel like I belong somewhere again."

Noah nodded, understanding in his eyes. "I know what you mean. After losing Colleen, I struggled to find my place. But being here, with

Lily and the church family, it's helped me heal in ways I never expected."

He reached out, his hand brushing against hers in a gesture of comfort and connection. Milly's breath caught at the contact, at the spark of electricity that seemed to pass between them.

For a moment, they stood there, lost in the shared understanding of grief and hope, of the unexpected ways that life could bring beauty from ashes. Then Noah smiled, a soft, gentle curve of his lips. "Come on," he said, "let's see if we can get this manger finished before the kids arrive for rehearsal."

Together, they turned back to their work, their hands moving in tandem as they crafted a scene of wonder and grace, a testament to the resilience of the human spirit and the power of love to heal even the deepest wounds.

5

The old wooden pews creaked as Milly settled beside her mother, the familiar scent of frankincense and polished wood stirring distant memories. Sunlight streamed through the stained-glass windows, casting a kaleidoscope of colors across the sanctuary. Her eyes wandered, taking in the evergreen wreaths and twinkling lights adorning the walls, until they landed on a familiar figure.

Noah stood on a ladder near the altar, his strong hands carefully draping garlands along the edge of the pulpit. His brow furrowed in concentration as he worked, a lock of dark hair falling across his forehead. Milly's heart skipped a beat, an unexpected warmth spreading through her chest.

"Doesn't the church look lovely?" her mother whispered, nudging Milly gently. "It's so nice to have you here with me."

Milly managed a small smile. "It's been a while, hasn't it? I forgot how peaceful it feels."

As the service began, Milly found herself sneaking glances at Noah, noticing the way his eyes crinkled at the corners when he smiled at his daughter beside him. A wave of longing washed over her, followed by a pang of guilt. She shouldn't be feeling this way, not here, not now.

Across the aisle, Noah tried to focus on the pastor's words, but his thoughts kept drifting to Sarah. He could almost feel her presence beside him, her hand warm in his. Lily leaned against his arm, her small voice joining in the hymns with unbridled joy. Noah envied her unwavering faith, wishing he could find that same solace.

As the congregation rose to sing, Noah's gaze met Milly's. For a moment, the world seemed to fade away, and he felt a flicker of something he hadn't experienced in years—a spark of connection, of possibility. But as quickly as it came, the moment passed, and Noah looked away, his heart heavy with the weight of his past.

After the service, Noah busied himself with tidying up, trying to ignore the twist of emotions in his gut. Lily bounded over to him, her eyes shining.

"Daddy, can we go to the park later? Please?" she pleaded.

Noah ruffled her hair affectionately. "Sure thing, sweetie. Let me just finish up here."

As he watched Lily skip away to join her friends, Noah couldn't help but glance over at Milly once more. She was helping her mother with her coat, her chestnut hair falling in soft waves around her face. A part of him longed to go to her, to strike up a conversation, but the guilt held him back.

"I miss you, Colleen," he whispered under his breath. "I don't know if I'm ready for this."

With a heavy sigh, Noah turned back to his task, the battle between his heart and his conscience raging on within him.

❄

As Noah stepped out of the church, the crisp autumn air filled his lungs. He paused for a moment, taking in the vibrant colors of the changing leaves, when a soft voice caught his attention.

"It's beautiful, isn't it?" Milly stood beside him, her hazel eyes fixed on the picturesque landscape. "I'd almost forgotten how peaceful it is here."

Noah nodded, a small smile tugging at his lips. "It's easy to get caught up in the bustle of life and forget to appreciate the little things."

They walked together in comfortable silence, their footsteps crunching on the fallen leaves. After a moment, Milly spoke again, her voice tinged with a hint of sadness.

"I used to find so much comfort in my faith, but after losing James, I just...I struggled to find my way back."

Noah's heart clenched at her words, a familiar pain resonating within him. "I understand," he said softly. "Losing Colleen shook my world. It's hard to reconcile that kind of loss with the idea of a loving God."

Milly glanced at him, her eyes shimmering with unshed tears. "How do you do it? How do you keep moving forward?"

"Lily," Noah answered without hesitation. "She's my reason, my anchor. Her faith is so pure, so unwavering. It reminds me that there's still good in this world, even when it feels like everything is falling apart."

A gentle breeze rustled through the trees, carrying with it the faint scent of chimney smoke. Milly pulled her coat tighter around herself, a shiver running through her.

"I wish I had that kind of strength," she murmured.

Noah stopped walking and turned to face her, his blue eyes earnest. "You do, Milly. I can see it in you. The fact that you're here, that you're trying...that takes courage."

A small, grateful smile played on Milly's lips. "Thank you, Noah. That means more than you know."

They resumed their walk, the church bells chiming in the distance. Noah felt a warmth spreading through his chest, a feeling he hadn't experienced in a long time. But as quickly as it came, doubt crept in, reminding him of the vows he'd made, the love he'd lost.

"I should probably head back," he said, his

voice tinged with reluctance. "Lily will be waiting for me."

Milly nodded in understanding, her own heart heavy with the weight of their shared struggles. "Of course. I...I'm glad we had this talk, Noah."

"Me too," he replied, his gaze lingering on hers for a moment longer than necessary.

As they parted ways, both Milly and Noah felt a bittersweet mix of hope and uncertainty. The connection they'd forged was undeniable, but the path forward was unclear, their hearts still tethered to the ghosts of their pasts.

6

Milly stood amidst a flurry of activity in the church's community center, a Santa hat perched lopsidedly on her chestnut waves. Around her, volunteers sorted through piles of donated coats, toys, and canned goods. The scent of pine needles and cinnamon wafted from the wreath on the door.

"Milly, dear, could you help Noah carry those boxes?" Her mother gestured toward a tall figure across the room, his broad shoulders straining as he lifted a heavy cardboard carton.

Milly hesitated, then nodded. As she approached, Noah looked up, his blue eyes crinkling at the corners. "Thanks for the help. These are heavier than they look."

Together, they hauled the boxes to the distribution tables. Milly couldn't help but notice the gentle way Noah handled each item, as if it were a precious gift. She found herself lingering, watching him work.

"Daddy, look what I made!" Noah's daughter bounded up, waving a glittery Christmas card. "It's for one of the kids."

Noah knelt to admire Lily's handiwork. "That's beautiful, sweetheart. I'm sure it will make someone very happy."

Lily turned to Milly, her eyes wide. "Do you think God will like it too? My Sunday school teacher said God loves it when we help others."

Milly's breath caught. How could she explain her tangled relationship with faith to this innocent child? She glanced at Noah, seeing the flicker of uncertainty in his eyes, and something shifted inside her. Kneeling beside Lily, Milly took the girl's small hands in hers.

"I think," Milly began softly, "that God is very proud of you for being so kind and thoughtful. Your card is going to make Christmas extra special for another little boy or girl."

Lily beamed, then scampered off to make more cards. Milly stood slowly, her heart full. She caught Noah watching her, a curious mix of emotions playing across his face.

As they worked side by side, packing boxes and sorting donations, Milly felt a warmth blossoming in her chest that had nothing to do with the busy room. It was a sense of purpose, of connection—to her community, to something greater than herself.

And maybe, just maybe, it was the first tentative step back toward the faith she'd left behind.

※

As the day drew to a close, Milly and Noah found themselves alone in the church's quiet sanctuary. The soft glow of candlelight cast a warm, comforting ambiance, and the distant echo of Christmas carols drifted through the air.

Milly sat in a pew, her hands clasped tightly in her lap. Noah hesitated for a moment before settling beside her, leaving a respectful distance between them. They sat in silence, each lost in their own thoughts, until Noah cleared his throat.

"I haven't been the best at praying lately," he admitted, his voice barely above a whisper. "It's been... difficult, since Colleen passed."

Milly nodded, understanding etched in her

features. "I know what you mean. After losing James, I felt like I couldn't find the words anymore."

Noah shifted slightly, turning to face her. "But today, seeing you with Lily, it made me realize that maybe I've been looking at it all wrong. Maybe it's not about finding the perfect words, but about opening our hearts."

A faint smile tugged at Milly's lips. "I think you might be right."

Slowly, tentatively, they bowed their heads together. At first, the silence stretched between them, awkward and heavy. But as they sat there, shoulders nearly touching, something began to shift.

Milly took a deep breath and allowed the words to flow from her heart. "Dear Lord," she whispered, "thank you for bringing us together today. For reminding us of the love and compassion that still exists in this world."

Noah's voice joined hers, low and earnest. "Please help us to find strength in each other, and in our faith. Guide us as we navigate these uncertain paths."

As they continued to pray, their words intermingling in the stillness of the sanctuary, Milly felt a sense of peace wash over her. It was as if a weight had been lifted from her shoulders, replaced by a glimmer of hope that had long been absent.

When they finished, Milly and Noah sat in comfortable silence, letting the tranquility of the moment envelop them. Milly glanced at Noah, noticing the way the candlelight softened his features, and felt a flutter in her heart that she hadn't experienced in years.

Perhaps, in this unexpected moment of shared vulnerability, they had found the first stepping stone on the path to healing. And as they left the sanctuary, shoulders brushing lightly, Milly couldn't help but wonder if this was just the beginning of something truly special.

7

Snowflakes drifted lazily from the gray December sky as Milly and Noah walked side by side through Cedar Ridge Park, their boots crunching on the fresh powder. Milly pulled her scarf tighter around her neck, savoring the comforting warmth. She glanced over at Noah, noticing how the snowflakes dusted his dark hair and clung to his long lashes.

"I haven't been back here since..." Milly's voice trailed off as painful memories threatened to surface. She swallowed hard. "Since James passed away."

Noah met her gaze, his blue eyes filled with understanding. "I'm sorry, Milly. Losing someone you love...it changes everything."

"You would know," she said softly. "How long has it been since...?"

"Two years now since Colleen died." Noah's voice was tinged with sorrow. "Some days it feels like a lifetime ago. Other times, it's like it just happened yesterday."

Milly nodded, blinking back tears. She understood that dichotomy all too well. The ache of missing James was a constant companion, even as life marched relentlessly forward.

As if sensing her thoughts, Noah reached out and squeezed her gloved hand. The simple gesture spoke volumes, conveying empathy and support without the need for words. Milly felt her heart swell with gratitude for this man who truly understood her pain.

They walked in companionable silence for a while, the only sounds the whisper of falling snow and the distant shouts of children playing. Milly found herself stealing glances at Noah, admiring the strong line of his jaw and the gentle curve of his lips. A flicker of something warm and unfamiliar stirred within her.

Feeling suddenly flustered, Milly pulled her hand from Noah's and tucked a stray lock of hair behind her ear. What was she doing? She couldn't let herself fall for him, no matter how kind and handsome he was. Her heart still belonged to James.

"I should probably get going," she said, her voice trembling slightly. "I promised my mom I'd help with the church bake sale."

Noah looked at her, his brow furrowed with concern. "Milly, is everything okay? Did I say something wrong?"

"No, no, it's not you." Milly shook her head vehemently. "I just...I don't think I'm ready for this. For us. It's too soon."

Understanding dawned in Noah's eyes, tinged with a flicker of disappointment. He took a step back, giving her space. "I get it, Milly. Believe me, I do. I'm not sure I'm ready either, to be honest."

Milly felt a pang of regret at the distance between them, both physical and emotional. But she knew it was for the best. They both needed time to heal before even considering opening their hearts again.

"I care about you, Noah," she said quietly. "But I think we both need to focus on ourselves right now. On our faith and finding peace with the past."

Noah nodded, a sad smile playing at the

corners of his mouth. "You're right. Lily needs me, and I need to be there for her. And you need time too."

They stood there for a long moment, snowflakes swirling around them in a delicate dance. Then Noah reached out and brushed a snowflake from Milly's cheek with a gentle finger.

"I'll be here if you ever need a friend, Milly. Don't forget that."

With those parting words, he turned and walked away, his tall form soon obscured by the falling snow. Milly watched him go, her heart heavy yet strangely hopeful.

Someday, perhaps, they would both be ready to love again. But for now, she would lean on her faith and cherish the budding friendship between two kindred spirits. Fate had brought them together in this season of joy and sorrow—only time would tell what the future held.

8

It had been days since Milly's last conversation with Noah, and for some reason, she couldn't get him off her mind.

So now, there she stood on the front porch of the Boyle house, her breath forming small clouds in the chilly air. She raised her hand to knock, but the door swung open before her knuckles could make contact. There stood Lily, her eyes bright and a wide smile on her face.

"Miss Milly! I've been waiting for you," Lily exclaimed, reaching out to grab Milly's hand and pull her inside. "I have something important to tell you."

Milly allowed herself to be led into the cozy living room, her heart warming at the sight of the twinkling Christmas tree and the crackling fire in the hearth. She settled onto the sofa, and Lily climbed up beside her, her small face serious.

"I've been praying for you, Miss Milly," Lily said solemnly. "Every night before bed, I ask God to help you feel better and to bring a smile back to your face."

Milly felt tears prick the corners of her eyes, touched by the little girl's heartfelt words. She reached out and pulled Lily into a gentle hug, whispering, "Thank you, sweetheart. That means more to me than you know."

From the doorway, Noah watched the exchange, his heart swelling with a mixture of emotions. He had been hesitant to pursue anything with Milly, afraid of the risk to his own fragile heart. But seeing the way Lily had taken to her, the way his daughter's simple faith had moved Milly to tears, made him wonder if perhaps their meeting was more than just chance.

As if sensing his presence, Milly looked up and met Noah's gaze. In that moment, a flicker of understanding passed between them—a recognition that the path forward might be uncertain, but it was one they could walk together, with faith as their guide.

Noah stepped into the room, his voice gentle as he said, "Lily's been talking about you non-stop, Milly. I think she's adopted you as an honorary member of the family."

Milly laughed softly, the sound mingling with Lily's delighted giggles. "I'm honored," she said, her eyes shining with a newfound warmth. "And I feel so blessed to have you both in my life."

As the three of them settled in to spend a cozy evening together, the earlier tensions and doubts seemed to melt away, replaced by a sense of belonging and the glimmering hope of a future where love and faith could heal even the deepest of wounds.

Lily hopped off the couch, her little face alight with excitement. "Daddy, can we show Miss Milly the special project we've been working on?"

Noah chuckled, ruffling his daughter's hair affectionately. "I don't see why not, pumpkin. Why don't you go grab it from the workshop while I put on some hot cocoa for us all?"

As Lily scampered off, Noah turned his attention to Milly, his blue eyes warm and inviting. "I hope you don't mind staying for a bit. Lily's been bursting at the seams to show you what we've been up to."

Milly shook her head, a soft smile playing on her lips. "I wouldn't miss it for the world. Besides, I could never say no to hot cocoa."

The sound of Lily's footsteps echoed through the house as she returned, carefully cradling a small wooden box in her hands. She placed it gently on the coffee table, her eyes shining with pride. "Go ahead, Miss Milly. Open it!"

With a curious glance at Noah, who nodded encouragingly, Milly reached out and lifted the lid. Inside, nestled on a bed of soft velvet, was a delicate wooden angel, its wings intricately carved and its face painted with the most serene expression. Milly's breath caught in her throat as she gingerly lifted the ornament from the box, marveling at the craftsmanship.

"Did you make this?" she asked softly, her gaze shifting between Noah and Lily.

Lily nodded enthusiastically. "Daddy helped me, but I did all the painting myself. It's just like the one we made to put on our tree for Mommy. Do you like it?"

Milly's eyes glistened with unshed tears as she replied, "I love it, Lily. It's the most beautiful thing I've ever seen."

Noah watched the exchange, his heart swelling

with a mixture of love and something else—something that felt suspiciously like hope. He cleared his throat, his voice slightly rough with emotion as he said, "Lily wanted you to have it, Milly. She said it would help you remember that you're never alone, that God and your loved ones are always watching over you."

A single tear escaped down Milly's cheek as she clutched the angel to her heart, overwhelmed by the gesture. "Thank you," she whispered, her voice trembling. "I'll treasure it always."

As Noah pressed a steaming mug of cocoa into her hands and Lily snuggled close to her side, Milly felt a warmth that had nothing to do with the crackling fire or the hot drink. It was the warmth of belonging, of being part of something special. And for the first time in a long while, she allowed herself to believe that maybe, just maybe, her broken heart could be whole again.

9

Glittering snowflakes drifted down from the darkening sky as Milly stood in the cozy warmth of the church foyer, her slender fingers trembling slightly as she adjusted the poinsettia arrangements. The scarlet blossoms blurred before her eyes, and she blinked back the tears threatening to spill over.

Today had been particularly hard. Some days were just worse than others, for no rhyme or reason.

Heavy footsteps approached and Milly turned to see Noah, his kind blue eyes filled with concern. "Milly? Is everything alright?"

She forced a watery smile. "I'm fine, really. It's

just...this time of year is hard, you know?" Her voice cracked on the last word.

Noah gently took her hands in his, his calloused palms warm and reassuring. "I understand," he said softly. "The holidays have a way of reminding us of what we've lost. But we're not alone in this, Milly. God is with us, even in our darkest moments."

As if on cue, the first notes of "Silent Night" drifted from the sanctuary, the melody achingly beautiful in its simplicity. Milly closed her eyes, letting the familiar words wash over her.

"Would you like to pray with me?" Noah asked, his voice barely above a whisper.

Milly nodded, and together they bowed their heads. Noah's deep, steady voice filled the space between them as he prayed for peace, for comfort, for the strength to carry on. Milly felt her own heart echoing his words, the weight of her grief slowly easing as she surrendered it to a higher power.

When they finished, Milly opened her eyes to find Noah watching her, his expression a mix of tenderness and understanding. In that moment, she felt a flicker of something she hadn't experienced in a long time—hope. Maybe, just maybe, she wasn't as alone as she'd thought.

❄

The next morning dawned crisp and clear, the freshly fallen snow blanketing the cemetery in a pristine white. Milly knelt beside the familiar headstone, her gloved fingers tracing the engraved letters of her fiancé's name.

"I miss you," she whispered, her breath forming frosty clouds in the chill air. "But I'm trying, I really am. I know you'd want me to find happiness again."

She closed her eyes, letting the peaceful stillness of the moment envelop her. For the first time in months, the ache in her chest felt a little less sharp, a little more bearable.

Across the cemetery, Noah stood before his wife's grave, his broad shoulders hunched against the cold. He'd watched Milly's quiet strength as she confronted her own loss, and it had inspired him to do the same.

"I'll never stop loving you," he murmured. "But our little girl needs her daddy to be whole again. I promise I'll try, for her sake and yours."

As if in answer, a gentle breeze stirred the bare branches overhead, carrying with it the faint scent of pine and the promise of new beginnings. Noah and Milly looked up at the same moment, their eyes meeting across the distance. And in that shared gaze, they found the courage to take the first step forward, out of the shadows of grief and into the light of hope.

❄

The winter sun hung low in the sky as Milly and Noah walked side by side through Cedar Ridge Park, their boots crunching on the frozen grass. They'd left the cemetery behind, both feeling lighter than they had in ages, as if a weight had been lifted from their shoulders.

Noah glanced at Milly, admiring the way her chestnut hair gleamed in the golden light. "I've been thinking," he began, his voice soft yet steady. "About the future, and what it might hold."

Milly met his gaze, her hazel eyes filled with a tentative hope. "Me too," she admitted. "It's been so long since I allowed myself to even consider a future without..." She trailed off, her breath catching in her throat.

Noah reached out, his calloused hand gently taking hers. "I know," he said, his thumb tracing soothing circles on her skin. "It's not easy, is it? Moving forward when a part of your heart will always be in the past."

Milly nodded, blinking back the tears that threatened to fall. "But I want to try," she whispered. "I felt God's presence today, at the cemetery. Like He was telling me it's okay to let go, to open my heart again."

"I felt it too," Noah confessed, a small smile tugging at the corners of his mouth. "And I realized that maybe, just maybe, He brought us together for a reason. Two broken hearts, learning to heal together."

They stopped walking, turning to face each other beneath the barren branches of an old oak tree. Milly's heart raced as she looked up into Noah's piercing blue eyes, seeing in them a reflection of her own longing and uncertainty.

"I don't know what the future holds," she said, her voice trembling slightly. "But I do know that I want to face it one step at a time, trusting in God's plan."

Noah's smile widened, his eyes crinkling at the corners. "One step at a time," he echoed, his free hand coming up to gently cup her cheek. "And with faith that He will guide us, every step of the way."

As they stood there, lost in each other's gaze, the first flakes of snow began to fall, swirling around them like a gentle benediction.

10

Multicolored lights illuminated the stage as the children of Cedar Ridge Community Church brought the Christmas story to life. Milly sat beside Noah in the hushed sanctuary, their shoulders gently brushing against each other. Her eyes followed the tiny wise men presenting their gifts to the newborn king, but her mind drifted to the man next to her.

As the play reached its crescendo, with the young actors raising their voices in a rendition of "Away In A Manger," Milly felt tears prick at the corners of her eyes. The familiar melody stirred something deep within her—a longing for the comfort and peace she once found in her faith.

Noah leaned in, his warm breath tickling her ear. "Are you alright?" he whispered, concern lacing his voice.

Milly nodded, offering him a watery smile. "Just feeling a bit nostalgic, I suppose. This play...it reminds me of simpler times."

Noah's hand found hers, his calloused fingers intertwining with her own. "I know what you mean. It's like a glimpse of hope, isn't it?"

They sat in companionable silence as the final notes of the carol faded away, the audience erupting into applause. Milly's heart swelled with a newfound sense of belonging, a realization that perhaps her journey had led her back to Cedar Ridge for a reason.

As the crowd began to disperse, Noah turned to Milly, his blue eyes shining with emotion. "Milly, there's something I need to tell you."

She tilted her head, curiosity mingling with a flutter of anticipation. "What is it, Noah?"

He took a deep breath, his grip on her hand tightening. "These past few months, getting to know you, spending time with you and Lily...it's meant more to me than I can put into words. I've been afraid to admit it, but I can't deny it any longer. Milly, I...I'm falling in love with you."

Milly's breath caught in her throat, her heart racing. She searched Noah's face, finding only sincerity and vulnerability etched into his handsome features. "Noah, I...I feel the same way. But I'm scared. We've both been through so much, and I don't want to rush into anything."

Noah nodded, a gentle smile tugging at his lips. "I understand. We can take things slow, let God guide us. All I know is that I want to walk this path with you, Milly, if you'll have me."

Tears spilled down Milly's cheeks as she threw her arms around Noah, burying her face in the crook of his neck. "Yes," she whispered, her voice thick with emotion. "Let's see where this journey takes us, together."

As they held each other in the softly lit church, Milly felt a wave of peace wash over her. For the first time in years, she allowed herself to imagine a future filled with love, laughter, and the unwavering support of a man who understood her heart. With Noah by her side and God's love guiding them, anything seemed possible.

❄

The sun rose on Christmas morning, casting a gentle glow through the frosted windows of Cedar Ridge. Milly stirred from her slumber, a smile already playing on her lips as she recalled the events of the previous evening. Noah's heartfelt confession and their mutual decision to embark on a relationship filled her with a warmth that rivaled the coziness of her quilted blanket.

She dressed quickly, eager to start the day and share in the joy of the holiday with those she held dear. As she stepped out onto the porch, the crisp winter air kissed her cheeks, invigorating her senses. The sound of crunching snow beneath her boots accompanied her as she made her way to the church.

Inside the sanctuary, the congregation gathered, their voices raised in hymns of celebration. Milly slipped into a pew beside Noah and Lily, her heart swelling with gratitude as Noah's arm draped around her shoulders, drawing her close.

Pastor Jacobs took to the pulpit, his eyes twinkling with the spirit of the season. "On this blessed Christmas morning," he began, his voice ringing out with conviction, "we come together to celebrate the greatest gift of all—the birth of our Savior, Jesus Christ. But let us also remember the gifts we have been given in each other, the love and support of our community, and the opportunity for new beginnings."

As the pastor spoke, Milly felt the last vestiges of her guardedness melt away. She leaned into Noah's embrace, marveling at the way their hearts seemed to beat in unison. Lily, nestled between them, looked up at Milly with adoration, her tiny hand reaching out to grasp Milly's own.

In that moment, surrounded by the love of her newfound family and the grace of God, Milly knew she was exactly where she was meant to be. The journey ahead would undoubtedly hold its share of challenges, but with faith as her guide and Noah's unwavering support, she felt ready to face whatever lay ahead.

As the service drew to a close, the congregation filed out into the crisp morning air, exchanging warm wishes and heartfelt embraces. Milly, Noah, and Lily walked hand in hand, their laughter carrying on the gentle breeze.

"Merry Christmas, Milly," Noah whispered, pressing a tender kiss to her temple.

"Merry Christmas, Noah," she replied, her eyes shining with the promise of a future filled with love, healing, and the eternal hope that Christmas morning brings.

And so, as the bells of Cedar Ridge chimed in joyous celebration, Milly and Noah stepped forward into their new beginning, their hearts open to the miracles that awaited them, both on this blessed day and in all the days to come.

EPILOGUE

A year later, the sun's first rays peeked through the stained-glass windows of the church, casting a kaleidoscope of colors across the pews. Milly, Noah, and Lily sat together, their hearts filled with a newfound sense of hope and belonging.

As the morning light danced across their faces, Milly's mind drifted back to the day she and Noah had exchanged vows in this very church. It seemed like a lifetime ago, yet the memories were as vivid as if it had happened yesterday. She remembered the way Noah's eyes had glistened with love and promise as he slipped the ring onto her finger, the way their hands had trembled as they joined together in prayer, and the overwhelming sense of peace that had enveloped them both.

In the year since their wedding, Milly, Noah, and Lily had grown together in ways she had never thought possible. The once-broken pieces of their lives had slowly mended, forming a beautiful mosaic of love, faith, and family. Milly had learned to open her heart again, to trust in the power of second chances, and to find joy in the simplest of moments.

She watched as Lily, now a year older and filled with boundless energy, snuggled between them on the pew. The little girl's laughter echoed through the church, a sound as sweet as the hymns that filled the air. Milly's heart swelled with love for this precious child who had become her own, and for the man who had given her the greatest gift of all—a family to cherish.

Noah's hand found hers, their fingers intertwining as if they were always meant to be. In his touch, she felt the strength and tenderness that had guided them through the challenges of the past year. Together, they had weathered storms of grief and uncertainty, but their love had only grown stronger, rooted in the solid foundation of their faith.

As the service began, Milly closed her eyes and offered a silent prayer of gratitude. She thanked God for the blessings that filled her life—for the love of a devoted husband, the laughter of a beautiful daughter, and the warmth of a community that had welcomed her home. In this moment, surrounded by the people she cherished most, Milly knew that she had finally found the peace and belonging she had always longed for.

The sunlight continued to stream through the stained-glass windows, painting the church in a kaleidoscope of colors—a perfect reflection of the vibrant love and joy that now filled their lives. Milly leaned her head on Noah's shoulder, content in the knowledge that, no matter what the future held, they would face it together, hand in hand, with faith and love guiding their way.

Lily, nestled between them, gazed up at the nativity scene with wide, wondering eyes. "Daddy, look! It's baby Jesus, just like in the play!"

Noah smiled down at his daughter, gently smoothing her hair. "That's right, sweetheart. And do you remember what the angel said? That Jesus came to bring us joy and peace."

Milly's heart swelled as she watched the tender exchange, marveling at the love and patience Noah showed his little girl. In that moment, she knew that whatever challenges lay ahead, they would face them together, as a family.

As the congregation rose to sing a hymn, Milly's voice joined the chorus, the words of praise and gratitude flowing freely from her heart. Noah's hand found hers, their fingers intertwining, and she felt a surge of strength and comfort in her new husband's touch.

The pastor's sermon spoke of new beginnings, of the transformative power of faith and love. Milly found herself hanging on every word, her spirit soaring with each passing minute. She glanced at Noah, finding his eyes already on her, shining with the same joy and contentment that filled her own heart.

When the service ended, the three of them lingered in the church, basking in the warmth of the community that surrounded them. As they made their way outside, Lily skipped ahead, giggling as she twirled in the fresh snow that blanketed the ground.

Noah wrapped an arm around Milly's waist, pulling her close. "Thank you for being here with us today," he murmured, his breath warm against her cheek.

Milly leaned into his embrace, savoring the feeling of his solid presence beside her. "There's nowhere else I'd rather be. This feels like home, Noah. You and Lily, this town, this faith...it's where I belong."

As they watched Lily play, her laughter ringing out like bells in the crisp winter air, Milly and Noah knew that they had found something precious: a chance to heal, to love, and to build a life together, guided by the light of God's unwavering grace.

EXCERPT FROM MAIDEN'S BLUSH

Terror filled her as she ran, stumbling across the snowy terrain. Her arms and legs stung from the icy wind whipping across them. She cried out as something sharp struck her. Pushing past the thorny branch, she felt the cut now upon her visage. As the tears trickled down her face, she felt the salty burn of them upon the fresh gash across her right cheek.

A roar sounded behind her, and she turned as the red Lexus skidded to a stop. A new panic seized her as she heard the door slam shut and saw the figure racing toward her. She turned and fled, faster than before, hoping she could make it to the road just ahead.

Hearing the deafening thumps of the steps

getting closer, she hazarded a look back. As she turned, the strap of one petite heel stuck on a low-lying branch, tripping her. She smashed to the frozen ground—hard. Jerking her foot from the shoe, she scrambled up, her hands stinging against the cold snow.

Halfway up, she felt a fierce tug from behind. Harsh hands gripped her waist. "Where do you think you're going?" The dark voice rasped in her ear.

She struggled, desperately trying to break away, but he was far too strong. She screamed, and his arms tightened across her body, one hand covering her mouth. She opened her mouth and sunk her teeth into his flesh as hard as she could. He cried out in pain, cursing, as she broke free.

She had barely gotten five feet away when he recaptured her. She turned, seeing the rage in his eyes.

Then, complete darkness engulfed her as she felt the blow across her face.

❄

Jack Barringer surveyed the sparkling landscape around him through the window of his dark blue

Corvette as he carefully sped along the road toward home . Despite the snowy landscape, the roads had been freshly plowed and were pretty clear.

The sky was sprinkled with stars, and the moon bathed the scenery with a picturesque glow. He turned up his radio. With the ground covered in a glittery white blanket, he could almost believe he really was in a winter wonderland. He rolled down his window for just a moment to feel the rush of the wind, deeply breathing in the cold, clear air. Ah, there was nothing like a Massachusetts winter.

It would be nice to be home for the holidays this year. Christmas was just a month away, and he had it planned to slow things down a bit and relax until the New Year. Business had been great lately. He could certainly afford to take some time off, and, besides, he needed the break.

He was among the best translators on the market, and the clientèle he served knew it. He was bilingual in six languages: Spanish, French, Italian, German, Russian, and Arabic. That's why he could do things on his terms. His father had spared no expense to ensure his son was afforded the very best education. He could still hear his cultured voice saying, "Trust me, son, this will all prove to be useful someday."

And, oh, how right he had been. Thanks to him, he had an extremely well-paying job and was allowed to travel the world at his ease. Just recently, he'd been asked if he'd ever considered giving speeches about how to achieve financial success. That would have better suited his father's expertise.

As the flurries upon his window became thicker, he clicked his windshield wipers on. If only he'd told his father how much he had appreciated everything. He was surprised to feel a sharp stab of pain at that thought. It'd been three years since his father's yacht had sunk, taking with it the only parent he'd ever known. At first, he'd been filled with helpless fury. Why his father who had been nothing but loving and kind to everyone? Why his father whose every intention had been to serve and glorify God?

He'd raged at the Almighty and pummeled him with unanswered questions until he'd finally realized that it was useless to be angry with him. After all, he was the Alpha and Omega, the beginning and the end. He had to know what he was doing. He must have a reason for all things. Jack ran a hand through his dark hair. He'd also learned that it did no good to dwell on the past either.

All memories put aside for now, he turned the next curve in happy spirits once more but then slowed as he spotted something lying on the ground on the left side of the road. He leaned forward and squinted through his window. It looked too large to be an animal—at least a domestic animal like a dog or a cat. He watched as part of the bundle jumped up and took off toward the shiny red Lexus he hadn't even noticed was there.

Warning bells began to go off in his head. What was this? He pushed his foot on the accelerator.

The door of the vehicle ahead slammed before the automobile took off down the road with a squeal.

Something wasn't right here. That man left with too much haste. Jack pulled his vehicle onto the side of the highway and stepped out.

The form upon the ground wiggled a bit as he started toward it. He heard a faint moan that sounded much like that of a woman. Wait a minute, a woman? His brows furrowed and his progress quickened. Alarm filled him as comprehension of what he had just witnessed dawned.

He knelt over the tiny body, oblivious to the wet snow seeping through his suit, and noted the red marks upon her face. Sympathy and anger imbued him. Sympathy for the poor victim. Anger at the heartless villain who would do such a thing. What man could possibly look himself in the mirror and not feel guilt over a crime such as this? How could a man ever physically hurt a woman and not feel shamed at his actions? He'd been raised to be a gentleman. Ingrained in him was the habit to treat all women with respect. He'd been taught early on never to strike a woman, even if angry. And that was one rule he'd always followed.

He squatted down and lightly touched her tiny wrist. She didn't move. She must have lost consciousness. He gently probed her joints. Nothing was broken at least. Although judging by the marks on her face, she would likely have bruises there and elsewhere.

She needed help, so of course he couldn't just leave her there. He put his arms under her and lifted her with ease, surprised at how light she was. Her long, golden hair fell away from her face and brushed his arms. She winced and cried out in pain. Her consciousness was returning. That was definitely a good sign.

Her lids shot open, revealing big blue eyes surrounded by thick lashes that cast shadows over her delicate cheeks. She screamed and struggled, her fists flying, but weakly. He barely blocked a swing to his mouth, capturing both her wrists in one hand, while still holding her with the other. "It's okay," he said soothingly. "I'm not going to hurt you.

I'm going to help you."

When she continued her vain attempt to escape, he turned her head towards him. "You're stuck out in the middle of nowhere. It's snowing, and if you don't find somewhere warm, you'll freeze to death. Trust me," he said gently. "What do you have to lose?" He wasn't sure if she understood what he was saying. She might have been in too much shock. Nevertheless, she stilled, and he carried her to his car on the side of the road.

❄

Katrina's heart pounded in her chest as the stranger secured her in the passenger seat of the Corvette and closed the door. She watched as he passed in front of the car and got in. He was tall—very tall, at least six inches taller than she was and had dark hair and eyes. He carried himself with the ease of someone who was wealthy and sophisticated. She gulped. Just like Bryan. She shook at the mere thought of him.

Bryan was her father's manager. Her father, David Weems, was a successful lawyer, and Bryan worked for him. He was her father's most trusted friend and helped him with many of his cases. She could see them now, heads bent together busily conversing, occasionally laughing and patting each other on the back. She grimaced. Her father thought of Bryan as the son he'd never had. He depended on him. He trusted him—too much.

She shivered violently. She couldn't remember ever being this cold in her life, wearing only her black evening gown and no shoes. She'd lost those in her flight. She wished she'd have had enough sense to grab her fur coat before jumping out of the car, though at the time her only thought had been to flee.

As if sensing her thoughts and sympathizing, the engine roared to life, and heat hit her face. The stranger in the driver's seat removed his coat and then reached across the car toward her. She recoiled back, eyes wide, scooting as close to the passenger-side door as she could get, prepared to jump from this car too if need be.

The man, apparently, seeing her fear, simply placed his coat on the middle console. "To warm you faster," he nodded toward the coat gently.

"Thank you," she barely managed with a lump in her throat. She took the coat and hugged it around her shoulders as the car began to move onto the road. Suddenly, a new thought struck her. Who was this man and where was he taking her? Panic seized her. What if he were just like Bryan? He'd said he would help, but so had Bryan. What if she had escaped Bryan only to end up with someone worse?

Her hands gripped the edges of her seat tightly. "Where are you taking me?" she asked, her voice shaky.

He glanced at her. "To the hospital," he answered. "I checked your joints. Nothing's broken, but you should still be checked out by professionals."

"No!" she croaked out. He momentarily took his eyes off the road to glance over at her again. "I can't go to the hospital," she fairly shook. Bryan was smart and resourceful. If she checked into a hospital, he would surely find her.

The stranger pulled the car onto the side of the road, and she stared at his huge hands as he shifted the gear in the middle of the car into park. She stared at him warily as his muscular frame turned toward her. "What's your name?" he asked.

She paused. How did she know she could trust this man? Frantic questions ran through her mind, and she licked her lips nervously, her eyes darting out the window frantically. They were in the middle of nowhere. There was nowhere for her to run. Of course, there hadn't really been anywhere for her to run when she'd jumped out of Bryan's car either. She'd just acted on instinct then.

She glanced back at the driver. He was her only means of getting help right now. He was right. If he hadn't shown up, she would have probably become even more lost than she already was and frozen to death. Looks like it was either take a chance and trust him or become a frozen statuette. She would have to trust him.

Besides, if he had intentions of hurting her, he would have acted on them already, wouldn't he?

"Katrina," she answered hesitantly, pressing closer into the seat.

He noticed the defensive gesture, and his voice softened. "I'm Jack Barringer. And I'm not going to harm you. I'm just going to take you to a hospital where you'll be properly cared for."

"I'm not going to a hospital," she stated defiantly with a hint of panic to her voice. He raised his brows and studied her. "I'm not," she repeated firmly, uncomfortable under his scrutiny but adamant in her reiteration.

He didn't question her, just started the engine. "Where are you staying? With family, at a hotel?" His steady gaze rested on her.

Her stomach plunged as the gravity of her situation fully hit her. Here she was in the middle of nowhere sitting in a car with a complete stranger and nowhere to go. No purse, no credit cards, no identification—nothing. She almost laughed at the absurdity of it all. She didn't even have any shoes. Who would have ever thought that she, Katrina Weems, the Harvard graduate, would ever have been so stupid as to screw up this bad?

Her face paled as she thought of how angry Bryan was sure to be. She could only imagine what his wrath would be like if he found her. He was probably right now rummaging through her purse. He would know even more about her than he already assuredly did. He now had her social security number, her resumes and job applications, her money, and not to mention what else. She shuddered to think of him delving in her suitcase.

Oh, why had she been so naïve as to believe that he was only doing her father a favor by coming to pick her up at the airport? Why couldn't her father have just dropped his meeting and come to get her himself? Why did she agree to take an interview in Boston instead of flying straight home to Tennessee from California? The questions kept reverberating throughout her brain when she was jerked back to the present.

"Huh?" she asked, startled.

"I was asking if you had anywhere to stay," he repeated.

She shifted uncomfortably. "Um, no, not exactly."

He flicked his turn signal on and glanced at her curiously. "No problem then. We'll just find you a hotel to spend the night in, and we'll sort through everything tomorrow."

"It's not that easy," she said nervously.

"Why not?" He frowned.

"I don't have anyone, and all of my belongings

—my purse, everything—are gone...with him," she explained uneasily.

❄

He looked over at her and for the first time realized that she carried nothing but the clothes on her back. He let out a sigh of frustration. Yes, he pitied her situation, but he was definitely not feeling up to being this caliber of a rescuer. Having a big heart, he did try to help people in need. The world could be a cruel place, especially to women. This poor girl was proof of that. He felt his indignation rise again at the injustice of what he'd glimpsed. But he'd had small gestures in mind. He'd hoped to take her home to safety and be on his merry way.

So much for a relaxing vacation. Here he was stuck with a young woman who had nothing with her and was now totally dependent on him. *Why now, Lord?* Almost immediately, he realized what a jerk he was being and was chastised by his Heavenly Father. How selfish could he be? This wasn't her fault. He certainly couldn't leave her high and dry and scared as she was. God had obviously placed him there at that moment to help her, and he knew that's what he would have to do.

How was he going to do anything to help someone who didn't even have any proof of who she was, though?

She put her head in her hands, that long, golden hair falling on either side. She looked miserable, her fancy dress torn and dirty. He guessed she was a very attractive woman when not so unkempt as she was now. It was easy to imagine that a man would notice her. But what exactly had happened to put her in the state she was in now?

Compassion and remorse filled him at his selfishness. She had refused to go to the hospital. Was she afraid of being found by her attacker? What exactly had occurred by the time he arrived on the scene? She had nowhere to go. No friends or family in the area, no hotel reservation. Had she been staying with this man? Or was it something else? He hadn't pressed her for answers. She'd been through a trying ordeal.

No, she didn't want to be in this predicament any more than he did. It was worse on her part. She was the one who had been assaulted and left out in the cold with nothing.

"Hey," he steadied the wheel with one hand and reached out to touch her shoulder with the other. Mistake. She jumped at the contact, and he winced, mumbling an apology. She physically gathered herself together and raised her head, looking like a lost little girl. It went straight to his heart. "It's going to be okay. I'll pay for each of us a room. We'll sort through everything in the morning." He smiled. "I had planned to stay a night in Boston before returning home anyway."

She looked at him with skepticism and apprehension before slowly nodding her head. "Thank you," she weakly managed before looking back down as if she were ashamed.

Get Maiden's Blush now!

ABOUT THE AUTHOR

Award-winning author Kayla Lowe writes women's fiction that explores complex themes with sensitivity and depth. Kayla's books delve into the intricacies of relationships, self-discovery, and resilience. From cozy love stories interspersed with a bit of faith to heartwarming tales of friendship and suspenseful novels of empowerment and heartbreak, her books illustrate the struggles specific to women.

When she's not churning out her next novel, you can find her with her feet in the sand and a book in her hand or curled up on the couch with her dogs.

Visit her website at www.authorkaylalowe.com.

ALSO BY KAYLA LOWE

<u>Series</u>

<u>Women of the Bible Fiction</u>

<u>Ruth</u>

<u>Esther</u>

<u>Rachel</u>

<u>Hannah</u>

<u>Deborah</u>

❄

<u>Charms of the Chaste Court</u>

A Courtship in Covent Garden

Whispers in Westminster

Romance in Regent's Park

Serenade on Strand Street

Treasure in Tower Bridge

❄

Sweet Honey by the Sea

The Beekeeper's Secret (Book 1)

A Royal Honeycomb (Book 2)

Bees in Blossom (Book 3)

Honeyed Kisses (Book 4)

Blooming Forever (Book 5)

❄

Strawberry Beach Series

Beachside Lessons (Book 1)

Beachside Lessons (Book 2)

Beachside Lessons (Book 3)

❄

Panama City Beach Series

Sun-Kissed Secrets (Book 1)

Sun-Kissed Secrets (Book 2)

Sun-Kissed Secrets (Book 3)

❄

The Tainted Love Saga

Of Love and Deception (Book 1)

Of Love and Family (Book 2)

Of Love and Violence (Book 3)

Of Love and Abuse (Book 4)

Of Love and Crime (Book 5)

Of Love and Addiction (Book 6)

Of Love and Redemption (Book 7)

❋

<u>Standalones</u>

Maiden's Blush

❋

<u>Poetry</u>

Phantom Poetry

Lost and Found

Milton Keynes UK
Ingram Content Group UK Ltd.
UKHW031023011224
451693UK00004B/502